The Oogas
on the Field

Written by
Denise M. Fleming, M.Ed.

Illustrated by
Lisa M. Sutton, MBA

Colored by
Laurel Berkel

The Oogas on the Field

Published by Clovercroft Publishing, Franklin, Tennessee

Illustrated by Lisa M. Sutton

Colorization and Interior Layout Design by Laurel Berkel

Printed in the United States of America

ISBN: 978-1-948484-16-9

Hi! I'm Shooga! I live on the planet, Benevolent. Do you know what "benevolent" means? It means to be kind to others. Here on our planet, we strive to live by the Blue Rule. I think it's called the Golden Rule on your planet. It says that we should treat others how we want to be treated.

My friends and I like to go to school to learn, and we love to play at the park with our friends. And when we aren't in the classroom or at the park, we like to have have a little friendly competition playing Oogarami on the playing field.

One Saturday morning, my dad and I set out to go to the playing field to play Oogarami with a bunch of other Oogas. Dad was going to coach the game.

As my dad and I walked, we reviewed the rules of the game.

"Rule number 1- Treat everyone with respect.
Rule number 2- Play fair.
Rule number 3- Try your best," I said.

"Oh, and we forgot the most important rule of all!" Dad exclaimed.

"The Blue Rule! Treat others how they want to be treated!" we shouted.

When we got to the field, most of the other Oogas were already there. Rooga and Tooga ran up to me.

"Hey Shooga! Ready to play some ball?" said Rooga excitedly.

"Yea!" I exclaimed.

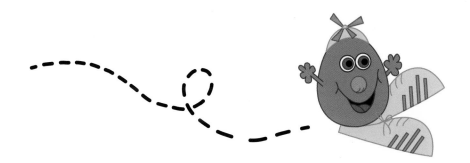

Coach blew his whistle and everyone ran to gather around him.
"Okay, Oogas, ready to play a game of Oogarami?"

"Yea!!!" everyone shouted.

Coach pointed at Rooga and me. "You two are the team captains
today. Rooga, you go over there, and Shooga, you go over there"
he said pointing to either side of him.

"Coach, Blooga won't be here today. He wasn't feeling well,
so his mom said he couldn't come and play," said one of the
players.

"That's okay," said Coach, "we'll just have an extra player on
one team."

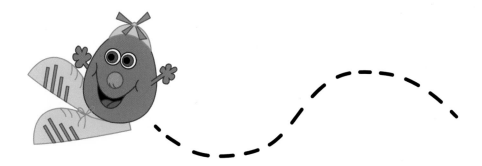

"Let's go over the rules of the game before we begin choosing teams," said Dad.

Everyone said the rules together:

"Rule number 1, Be respectful; Rule number 2, Play fair; Rule number 3, Play your best; and the most important rule of all: Treat Others As They Want to Be Treated!"

14

Rooga and I took turns choosing players for our teams.
Everything was going well until it came to the last player left.

Tooga stood there shyly as Rooga and I started to argue.

"Shooga, you can have Tooga. Our team will be fine with one less player," said Rooga.

"Ohhhh noooo, Rooga. We don't need Tooga like your team needs Tooga! You go ahead and take him," I firmly told him.

The arguing continued back and forth as Coach started to step in and take control and Tooga quietly started to walk away.

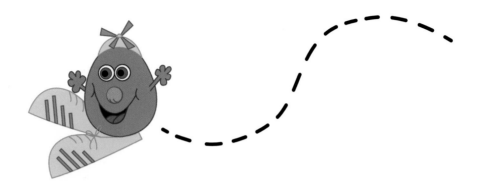

Coach called, "Tooga, where are you going?"

"It's okay, Coach. I didn't really want to play today. I'll just sit on the bleachers and watch the teams play," Tooga replied.

"You have just as much right to play as any of the other Oogas that are here!" Dad said with a stern voice.

"That's okay, I'd rather watch them and learn how to play the game better," said Tooga as he slowly walked towards the bleachers with his head turned slightly downward.

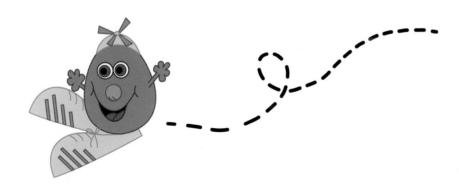

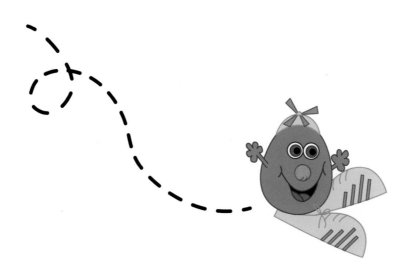

The teams gathered around Rooga and me to plan out our moves. While we played the game, my dad went over to Tooga and sat on the bleachers next to him.

"Hey, Tooga, are you sure you didn't want to play Oogarami today?" my dad asked him.

"Coach, no one really wanted me on their team. I didn't want to force anyone to have to pick me," said Tooga sadly.

Dad turned to Tooga and said, "Tooga, you are the only Ooga in this game that followed the most important rule of the game— The Blue Rule."

Coach patted Tooga on the back, got up, and went back to the game with the intention of having a little talk with the other Oogas after the game.

26

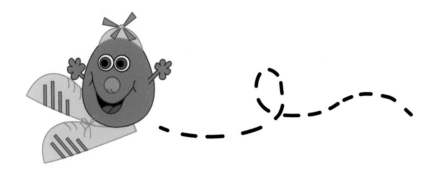

Tooga watched the game, cheered for both teams, and encouraged whoever had the ball. As the game was winding down, Tooga quietly got up and walked home, alone.

After the game, Coach gathered us all around him and asked everyone to go over the rules of the game again together. Everyone shouted, "Rule number 1, Treat everyone with respect; Rule number 2, Play fair; Rule number 3, Play your best; and the most important rule of all: Treat others as you want to be treated."

"Okay," said Coach, "which rule do you think could've been followed better today?" Dad was really good about not pointing fingers at who was at fault, but encouraged us to reflect on our words and actions that we chose to use.

We all quietly reflected on our words and actions of the day. I glanced over at Rooga at the same moment he glanced over at me. We both remorsefully walked toward my dad and together said, "We didn't follow The Blue Rule very well today."

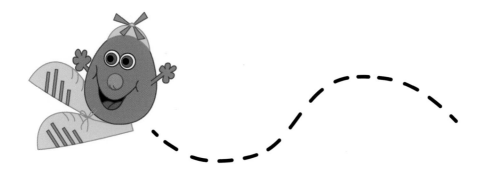

"Tell me how you didn't follow The Blue Rule," instructed Dad.

"Well, when we were arguing about who had to have Tooga, that isn't how I would want to be treated," said Rooga.

"Yea, I wouldn't want someone to make me feel unwanted for a game that is supposed to be about fun," I said sadly.

Coach started to smile and said, "What do I say is the most important thing about making a mistake?"

"To learn from them," said everyone in unison.

"Excellent!" said Coach. "Okay, everyone, great game. Same time and place next week."

All the Oogas started to gather their things while Rooga and I went over to talk with my dad. "Dad, we feel really bad about how we treated Tooga," I said.

"We all make mistakes and let our pride affect our choices, but we also have to forgive ourselves when we realize that we made a mistake," Dad said. I asked Dad if it would be okay if I walked home with Rooga and he said yes.

Rooga and I gathered our things and began walking home. As we walked home, we discussed a plan for next week's game.

The following week we were on the field again about to play Oogarami. Earlier I had asked my dad if I could be a team leader again. When we got to the field and began picking teams, my first pick was Tooga and my second pick was Rooga.

As we started to walk out to the field, I said, "Tooga, you were the best player on the team last week!"

Tooga looked at me strangely and said, "Shooga, I didn't play last week."

"You were as much a team player as any of us," I said. "You followed every rule AND modeled them for us to follow; we just didn't listen."

A smile came across Tooga's face as they got to the field.

46

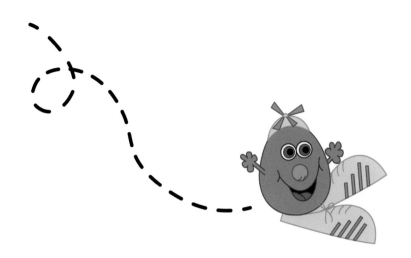

On the way home, Dad said to me, "Shooga, I'm very proud of you for how you treated Tooga today! He played better than he ever did, and I think that was because you helped his confidence in himself."

"Thanks, Dad," I said, "but I was only following The Blue Rule."

Discussion

1. Do you think it's important to reflect on your words and actions? Why or why not?

2. Which do you think is more important—fun or competition? Why?

3. Do you think it's just as important to forgive yourself as it is to forgive others? Why?

4. Why is it important to learn from your mistakes?